MY FIRST
PUPPY

I believe that owning a dog is one of the most
special relationships that a person can have.
They provide us with unconditional love, friendship
and loyalty. My son adores our dogs Nelson and Lucas —
he helps me feed, brush and play with them. It's
heartwarming to watch the joy that the three of them
give each other. When children are directly involved in
the care of their pet, the animal and child learn to respect
each other. I hope that this book provides children with an
insight into being a responsible pet owner so that we can
give our dogs the wonderful lives they deserve.

Lisa Chimes

For Brad, Hudson and our beautiful dogs, Nelson and Lucas
– LC

First American Edition 2016
Kane Miller, A Division of EDC Publishing

Text copyright © Lisa Chimes 2015
Illustrations copyright © Tina Burke 2015

First published by Penguin Group (Australia), 2015

For information contact:
Kane Miller, A Division of EDC Publishing
PO Box 470663
Tulsa, OK 74147-0663
www.kanemiller.com
www.edcpub.com
www.usbornebooksandmore.com

Library of Congress Control Number: 2015954248

Manufactured by Regent Publishing Services, Hong Kong
Printed March 2016 in ShenZhen, Guangdong, China

1 2 3 4 5 6 7 8 9 10

ISBN: 978-1-61067-516-1

MY FIRST PUPPY

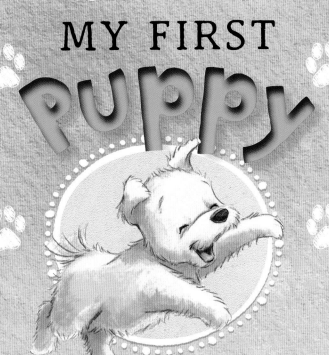

Dr. Lisa Chimes

Illustrated by Tina Burke

Kane Miller
A DIVISION OF EDC PUBLISHING

It was only twenty more sleeps until Sam's birthday.
He was turning five and all he wished for was his very own puppy.

He found his favorite dog book, the one with all the different kinds,
to show to Mom and Dad.

"Please can I have a puppy? Please? I like this one, Mom.
Look at his shaggy hair!"

Mom smiled. "That one grows very big, Sam. He might not be the right kind of dog for us. It's very hard work owning a dog. They need to be looked after every day."

Sam's dad nodded. "But if you learn a lot about dogs and how to care for a puppy, maybe we will get you one of your very own."

"Okay, I will learn everything. I promise," shouted Sam. "I'm going to be the best dog owner ever!"

Sam sat on the couch with Mom and they read lots of books about dogs.
They wrote a list of all the things a puppy needs.

Give your puppy:

- Lots of love and cuddles
- Daily exercise
- Toilet training
- Training to "sit" and "stay"
- Annual visits to the doctor
- A safe house and yard

Things a puppy needs:

- Puppy food and fresh water
- Food and water bowls
- Puppy toilet training pads or newspaper
- A dog bed, kennel or puppy crate
- Flea, worm and heartworm medicine
- A collar and leash
- A dog seat belt for the car
- Shampoo and a brush
- Toys

Sam learned all about the many different types of dogs.
He showed his favorites to Mom and Dad.

Cavalier King Charles spaniels are small dogs with medium-length silky coats and long fluffy ears. They were named after an English king who owned them and were bred to be companion dogs. They are sweet, fun-loving and social.

Labradors are medium-sized dogs with short, smooth, water-resistant coats. They originally worked as fishermen's dogs because they could retrieve things from water and work in very cold weather. Now they often work as service dogs. They are easygoing, loveable and highly trainable.

Collies are medium to large dogs with coats that are either long-haired or short. They were originally bred as herding dogs and sheep dogs, but the long-haired collie is most famous for being "Lassie" in the TV series, movies and books. They are patient, loyal and friendly.

Pugs are small dogs with short coats, a tightly curled tail and a flat snout that makes them "snuffle." They were originally bred in China and have been owned by royal families and celebrities all over the world. They are playful, confident and affectionate.

Beagles are small to medium dogs with long, soft ears and short, smooth coats. They have worked as hunters' dogs and tracking dogs, thanks to their very strong sense of smell. Now they often work as detection dogs. They are good-natured, clever and determined.

Dachshunds are small dogs with long bodies and short legs. They have short, long or wiry coats. Their name means "badger dog" in German and they originally worked as hunters' dogs because they could fit into holes and burrows. They are brave, smart and outgoing.

Bichons Frisés are small dogs with a curly coat that grows long unless it is clipped. Over the centuries they have been both companion dogs for European royalty and street dogs who performed with buskers or in the circus. They are happy, independent and cheeky.

Greyhounds are tall, slim dogs with short, smooth coats. For the last hundred years they have mostly been bred for sprint racing as they are very fast and love to chase, but their natural inclination is to sleep most of the day. They are sensitive, gentle and calm.

Standard poodles are medium to large dogs with a curly coat that needs to be clipped. They have been companion dogs and performing dogs, but originally they worked with duck hunters because of their ability to swim. They are charming, intelligent and eager to please.

"Some dogs love to sit on your lap," Sam said. "Others like to swim, run and chase balls. Dogs' hair can be long, short, curly, fluffy or flat. Some dogs have a lot of hair. Some don't. Some dogs are much bigger than me and others are so small they can fit in my arms."

So Mom and Dad took Sam to the dog shelter to find a puppy.

"This is where the dogs without families go," said Mom.

When Sam walked in, there was a lot of barking. There were so many dogs to choose from. There were big dogs, small dogs, fat dogs and skinny dogs. They were all different colors too.

"Remember, we might not find the right puppy today," said Mom. "We might have to be very patient."

When approaching a puppy for the first time, be very quiet. Kneel down to the puppy's level with your hand out. Don't approach the puppy too quickly or it might become frightened. Wait for the puppy to come and sniff your hand, then gently pat it on its back. Always ask the owner before approaching a dog you don't know.

But Sam spotted a small white puppy.
He had big brown eyes and little floppy ears.

Sam gave the puppy a cuddle and felt his soft, fluffy coat.

"Pleeeease, Mom and Dad! He's perfect for us.
Please, can we take him home?" he asked.

Mom and Dad looked at each other and then smiled at Sam.

"You're right, Sam," said Dad.

"He'll be perfect," said Mom. She gave Sam a hug.

Sam was so happy. He jumped up and down and then patted the puppy and gave him a kiss on the head.

"What will you call him?" asked Dad. "What about Max? Or Freddy?"

Sam gave the puppy a toy. The puppy pounced on it and said, *Rowf*.

Sam laughed. "That's it," he said. "Ralph! I'll call him Ralph."

When Sam got home he gathered all the things that Ralph needed.

Then he chose some toys for Ralph to play with.

Ralph loved his new toys and chewed them with his sharp little teeth.

"Good boy, Ralph," said Sam.

When Sam played with Ralph, he sometimes chewed at Sam's fingers.

"Ouch! Here, Ralph, chew your toy not my hand!"

Toys are important to stop puppies chewing other things like shoes or the furniture. Their teeth are still growing and they need to chew. Sometimes puppies will play-bite. This is normal. If your puppy nips you, yelp loudly. Remember to praise your puppy for gentle play. Training puppies to be well behaved should start when they are very young. Puppy preschool is a fun place where puppies and their owners get together to teach puppies good manners.

It had been a long day and Sam and Ralph were getting tired.
Sam put his pajamas on and crossed off a day on his countdown chart.

"Only two sleeps to go until my party," he said.

"Ralph might be scared by himself, Mom. Can he sleep in my room?
I can put the puppy crate on the floor near my bed. Please?"

"Okay, Sam, but he might keep you awake all night crying," said Mom.

That night, Ralph only cried for a few minutes.

And he was so happy to see Sam in the morning.

Puppies don't like to go to the bathroom near their bed or food, so always make sure to keep these separate. Some puppies sleep in a laundry room or in a kennel.

Mom, Dad and Sam started toilet training Ralph that day. They took Ralph outside as often as they could.

There were lots of accidents inside, so they put down some toilet training pads.

When your puppy has an accident inside, take them straight outside. Give your puppy a treat when they go to the bathroom there. If your puppy goes on the training pads or newspaper inside, give them a treat. Watch your puppy for any signs that they need to go to the bathroom — like sniffing — and show them where to go.

Never punish a puppy for having an accident inside — they are still learning. You need to give them a reward when they do the RIGHT thing.

"Good boy, Ralph! Here's a treat," said Sam, when Ralph went to the bathroom in the right place.

"You're doing a great job training him, Sam," said Dad. "But remember that toilet training can take a long time."

The next day was Sam's party. Sam blew out the five candles on his chocolate cake and everyone sang "Happy Birthday." The cake was delicious!

Ralph stood under the table, wagging his tail and licking his lips. He wanted some cake too!

"Mom, can I give Ralph a piece of cake?" Sam asked.

"Darling, chocolate is poisonous for dogs," said Mom. "We must never give him chocolate."

Sam looked down at Ralph. "No chocolate for you," he said.

Ralph looked sad, so Sam gave him a cuddle.

"Sorry," he said. "But I have to look after you."

There are lots of things in the home that can make your puppy sick if it eats them. Things like medicines, onions, avocado, grapes, raisins, chewing gum, cooked bones and even some clothes and small toys should be kept away from puppies.

Later, Sam went with Mom, Dad and Ralph to the vet.

Dr. Lisa checked Ralph and gave him a shot called a vaccination.

A vaccination is a special medicine that stops an animal from getting sick with certain diseases. Your puppy will also be spayed or neutered when they are older so they can't have babies, and will be microchipped, which is when a pellet is put under your puppy's skin with a big needle. If your pet is ever lost, scanning the chip will mean that a vet can contact you. It only hurts for a second, and it helps to keep your puppy safe.

She said that Ralph would need a checkup every year to keep him healthy.

Ralph looked frightened at the vet, so Sam gave him a pat to make sure he was okay.

Dr. Lisa showed Sam how to check Ralph every day to make sure he stayed healthy. Sam looked at Ralph's eyes, ears, nose, mouth and skin. He now knew how to check that Ralph was eating, drinking and going to the bathroom normally. If Sam noticed anything wrong, they should take him to the vet right away.

CHECKLIST

☑ **EYES**
clear with no redness or gunk around them

☑ **NOSE**
smooth and clean

☑ **EARS**
clean with no redness or bad smell

☑ **MOUTH**
white teeth, pink gums and no bad teeth

☑ **SKIN**
no flaky skin, no lumps and a shiny, even coat

Dr. Lisa said that when Ralph had finished all his shots in a few weeks, he could visit the park to play with other dogs.

Sam practiced using the leash at home. Ralph was confused at first and kept chewing on it.

When you hold the leash, put your hand through the strap and then grip the leash below the strap so that it can't slip off. Don't pull on the leash. Teach your puppy to walk next to you by giving it treats. Encourage your puppy to sit often while on the leash. Keep the training sessions short and fun. All dogs need exercise, just like people do. It keeps them healthy and happy. Your puppy should have at least thirty minutes of exercise every day — a walk on the leash, running at the dog park or even swimming.

When Sam took him off the leash, Ralph was so excited that he ran around in circles.

"He's so fast!" shouted Sam, laughing.

Sam taught Ralph to sit. He held a treat above Ralph's nose and then moved it over his head until Ralph's nose pointed to the sky.

"Sit," Sam said.

When Ralph sat, Sam gave him the treat right away.

"Good boy!" he said. "I'm going to practice this with you every day so you don't forget." Sam couldn't wait to teach Ralph to fetch a ball.

At the end of the day, Sam helped Mom give Ralph a bath for the first time. They used a special puppy shampoo that smelled like baby powder. Sam made sure he kept it out of Ralph's eyes.

Ralph looked funny all wet. He shook himself and sprayed water all over Sam.

Mom dried Ralph with a towel. "We better dry inside his ears to make sure they don't get sore," she said.

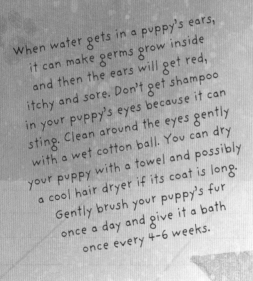

When water gets in a puppy's ears, it can make germs grow inside and then the ears will get red, itchy and sore. Don't get shampoo in your puppy's eyes because it can sting. Clean around the eyes gently with a wet cotton ball. You can dry your puppy with a towel and possibly a cool hair dryer if its coat is long. Gently brush your puppy's fur once a day and give it a bath once every 4-6 weeks.

After the bath, Sam gently brushed Ralph's soft white fur.
Ralph wagged his tail – he loved being brushed.

It had been a long day and Sam and Ralph were very tired.
Sam held Ralph on his lap and rubbed his warm tummy.

"I love you so much, Ralph. You're my best friend in the whole
world," he whispered.

Ralph gently licked Sam's hand and closed his eyes.

Sam smiled. He knew that Ralph loved him too.